I0764390

Schalken the Painter

A Gothic Tale of Artistic Obsession and Unholy Bargains

A Modern Translation

Adapted for the Contemporary Reader

J. Sheridan Le Fanu

Translated by Tim Zengerink

Table of Contents

Preface - Message to the Reader

What If You Could Help Rebuild the Greatest Library in Human History?

Thousands of years ago, the Library of Alexandria stood as the crown jewel of human achievement — a sanctuary where the collected wisdom of every known civilization was gathered, preserved, and shared freely.

And then, it was lost.

Through fire, conquest, and the slow erosion of time, humanity lost not just books — but ideas, dreams, discoveries, and stories that could have changed the world forever.

Today, the Library of Alexandria lives again — and you are invited to be a part of its restoration.

Our mission is simple yet profound:

To rebuild the greatest library the world has ever known, and to translate all timeless works into every language and dialect, so that no seeker of knowledge is ever left behind again.

By joining our movement to rebuild the modern Library of Alexandria, you become part of an unprecedented mission:

- **Unlimited Access to the Greatest Audiobooks & eBooks Ever Written:**

  Instantly explore thousands of legendary works—Plato, Shakespeare, Jane Austen, Leo Tolstoy, and countless more. All instantly available to read or listen, placing a complete literary universe at your fingertips.

- **Beautiful Paperback & Deluxe Editions at Printing Cost**

  Own any title as an elegant paperback, deluxe hardcover, or stunning collectible boxset—offered to you at true printing cost, delivered straight to your door. Build your personal Library of Alexandria, crafted for beauty, built for durability, and worthy of proud display.

- **Fresh Translations for Modern Readers—in Every Language & Dialect**

  Enjoy timeless masterpieces reimagined in clear, contemporary language—no more outdated phrases or obscure references. Alongside the original versions, we're tirelessly translating these classics into every language and dialect imaginable, ensuring accessibility and understanding across cultures and generations.

- **Join a Global Renaissance of Literature & Knowledge**

  You directly support expanding our library, publishing deluxe editions at true cost, translating works into all global languages, and bringing humanity's greatest stories to people everywhere. By joining today, you're not just preserving a legacy of masterpieces; you set in motion a powerful wave of literary accessibility.

Become a Torchbearer of Knowledge.

Join us for free now at **LibraryofAlexandria.com**

Together, we will ensure that the light of human wisdom never fades again.

With gratitude and a shared love of knowledge,

The Modern Library of Alexandria Team

Visit:

www.libraryofalexandria.com

Or scan the code below:

Introduction

Art, Repression, and the Gothic Specter of Possession

J. Sheridan Le Fanu's Schalken the Painter, first published in 1839 and later revised in his 1851 collection Ghost Stories and Tales of Mystery, is a haunting work of psychological and supernatural fiction. Blending elements of the traditional ghost story with a deep study of unspoken desire, religious dread, and moral compromise, the tale demonstrates Le Fanu's unmatched ability to create a world in which the real and the unreal interpenetrate with eerie ease. Set in the dark and shadowed streets of seventeenth-century Holland, the story weaves a spectral allegory of ambition, loss, and the inescapable reach of the infernal.

The protagonist, Godfrey Schalken, is a young and talented pupil of the Dutch master painter Gerard Douw. While apprenticing under Douw, Schalken falls in love with his master's beautiful niece, Rose. Their romance, however, is cut short when a mysterious suitor named Vanderhausen appears, offering great wealth in exchange for Rose's hand. Although his appearance is unnerving—cadaverous, silent, and cold—Douw is seduced by the money and agrees to the match, despite Rose's terror. She is wed to Vanderhausen and vanishes into the night. What follows is a series of increasingly bizarre and disturbing encounters, culminating in a spectral return and the gradual destruction of all who have come under Vanderhausen's shadow.

On the surface, Schalken the Painter is a tale of demonic possession, a Faustian bargain, and ghostly vengeance. But beneath its supernatural exterior lies a more complex psychological and thematic core. Le Fanu explores not only the supernatural, but also the social and emotional structures that enable evil: the commodification of women, the corruption of artistic ambition, and the moral cowardice of those who remain silent in the face of horror. It is a story of choices not made, of words not spoken, and of a love that cannot protect.

This introduction will explore the major themes, structure, and cultural context of Schalken the Painter, examining its place within Le Fanu's broader literary oeuvre and the gothic tradition as a whole. We will consider how the story reflects the tensions between desire and restraint, art and commerce, spiritual salvation and damnation. Through its subtle horror, Le

Fanu delivers not only a ghost story, but a parable of eternal consequences.

The Painter, the Muse, and the Bargain of Silence

Le Fanu's choice to base his story around a real historical figure—Godfried Schalcken, a painter known for his candlelit scenes and chiaroscuro technique—is no accident. The setting is steeped in the aesthetics of shadows, not only literally through the painter's use of light and dark, but metaphorically through the characters' moral ambiguity and emotional repression. In the world of the story, light is never clean or pure—it is always flickering, partial, and uncertain. This mirrors the characters' ethical vision, especially that of Schalken himself, who is presented as talented but impotent in the face of evil.

Schalken's failure is not one of ignorance, but of inaction. He loves Rose, and yet when she is handed over to the repulsive Vanderhausen, he offers no resistance. He is a man shaped by form, not courage—trained to observe, to render, to copy. His silence condemns both himself and the woman he adores. Even after Rose vanishes into the clutches of a man who is plainly otherworldly, Schalken does not pursue her or challenge his master's decision. His emotional passivity, like Douw's greed, creates a moral vacuum into which the supernatural rushes.

Rose, meanwhile, is the most tragic figure in the story. She is caught between two men who objectify her in different ways—Schalken through romantic idealization and Douw through mercenary transaction. Her resistance to Vanderhausen is heartfelt and desperate, yet no one listens. When she reappears, pale and broken, her presence is ghostly not just because she may be dead, but because her humanity has been erased by the choices of those around her. She is a symbol of violated innocence and the price of moral compromise.

Vanderhausen himself is a masterstroke of horror. Le Fanu offers almost no backstory, no origin, and no explanation for the suitor's existence. His unnatural stillness, his cold touch, and his ability to control others through sheer presence mark him as something not merely inhuman, but anti-human. He represents a force outside of normal life, one that invades through legal contracts and social conventions. His horror is bureaucratic: he marries through formal proposal, pays in coin, and vanishes with all the trappings of propriety. But behind that shell is something deathless and insatiable.

In this way, the story critiques not just individual actions, but systemic failures. Vanderhausen is allowed in not through force, but through willingness—because the world around him values wealth over well-being. It is a gothic indictment of a world that sells its soul not in blood, but in ink and silence.

Art as Witness, and the Haunting of Memory

As the story nears its conclusion, Schalken sees Rose once more—now a spectral figure, clothed in white, silently beckoning him into the shadows of a church. There, in a nightmarish vision, he finds her chained beside her demonic husband, forced to endure an eternity of torment. The scene is not an exorcism or a climax of combat, but a revelation. Schalken sees the result of his failure—not only Rose's suffering, but his own damnation in the form of regret. He flees and faints, powerless.

Yet Le Fanu does not allow him to forget. In the tale's final moments, Schalken is said to be haunted by the vision for the rest of his life, his art taking on a darker, more haunted tone. This is Le Fanu's final irony: the painter becomes famous not for his skill, but for his suffering. His light and shadow are no longer technique—they are trauma. His paintings, which once sought to capture beauty, now reflect horror. Art, in this case, becomes a kind of tombstone—a marker of memory, loss, and the things that cannot be undone.

Le Fanu draws here on the gothic tradition of memory as curse. The past does not pass. It lingers, reasserts, and corrupts. The haunting in Schalken the Painter is not merely supernatural; it is emotional, psychological, and artistic. The painter cannot forget what he saw because what he saw is the consequence of his own inaction. He did not cause Rose's fate, but he did nothing to prevent it. And in the world of gothic horror, omission is often as grave as commission.

This final turn also inverts the romantic myth of the suffering artist. Schalken's greatness is not inspiration—it is punishment. His legacy is built not on vision, but on failure. Every canvas, every flicker of light and shadow, becomes a quiet scream. And in this inversion, Le Fanu turns the gothic into a moral fable: art cannot redeem what conscience will not defend.

Conclusion:
Possession, Passivity, and the Gothic Legacy

Schalken the Painter endures because it is more than a ghost story. It is a meditation on complicity, on love turned powerless, and on the price of beauty when it is divorced from bravery. Le Fanu understood that the gothic is not simply about dark castles and shrieking phantoms—it is about the slow erosion of the soul under the pressure of silence, greed, and fear.

In this tale, the supernatural is not the disruption of reality—it is the fulfillment of its logic. A world that allows Vanderhausen in, that turns a woman into currency and leaves her unprotected, is already haunted. The ghost simply reveals what was always there.

The story's structure, told as a kind of painter's legend, adds to its power. It feels like a moral parable passed down through generations—one meant not merely to entertain, but to instruct. And its message is chillingly clear: If you remain silent in the face of evil, it will return. It will claim the innocent. And you will carry its shadow forever.

With Schalken the Painter, Le Fanu offers one of the most elegantly restrained yet emotionally devastating stories in gothic literature. It is a tale of ghostly return, yes—but also of love's failure, art's burden, and the haunting power of things left unsaid.

Strange Event in the Life of Schalken the Painter

You'll probably be surprised, my friend, by the story I'm about to tell you. What connection could I possibly have with Schalken—or him with me? He had gone back to his home country and was likely dead and buried before I was even born. I've never been to Holland, and I've never spoken to anyone from there. I think you already know that much. So I'll explain where I got this story from and why I believe it's true.

When I was younger, I knew a man named Captain Vandael. His father had served under King William both in the Netherlands and in Ireland. I don't know exactly why I liked being around him, since we didn't share the same views or religion—but I did. And it was through the trust we built during our friendship that I came to hear the strange story I'm about to tell you.

Whenever I visited Vandael, I couldn't help noticing a painting in his home. I'm not an art expert, but even I could tell there was something unusual about it. The way light and shadow were used was different, and the scene itself was odd enough to make me curious. The painting showed a room, maybe part of an old church. In the front stood a woman dressed in white, part of her outfit pulled up like a veil. The style wasn't like anything a nun would wear, but it still had a religious feel. She was holding a lamp, which was the only light in the scene, and her face had a mischievous smile, like someone who was playing a clever trick. In the background, barely lit by the dim red glow of a dying fire, stood a man dressed in old-fashioned clothes. He looked alarmed, with one hand on the hilt of his sword, as if he were about to draw it.

"Some paintings," I told Vandael, "just feel real. It's like they're not made-up scenes from the artist's imagination, but something that actually happened. That's how I feel about this one."

Vandael smiled and looked thoughtfully at the picture. Then he said, "You're not wrong. That painting shows a true and very strange event. Schalken painted it himself, and the woman in the picture is Rose Velderkaust, the niece of Gerard Douw. She was Schalken's first love—maybe his only one. My father knew Schalken personally and heard the whole story from him. This painting shows a scene from that story. It's considered one of Schalken's best works. The painting was left to my father in Schalken's will."

All I had to do was ask, and Vandael was happy to share the story behind the painting. That's how I came to know it—and now I can pass it on to you. You can decide for yourself whether or not to believe it, but I'll add this: Schalken was an honest, straightforward man, not someone likely to make up wild stories. And Vandael, who told me the tale, clearly believed every word.

Now, Schalken might not seem like the kind of person you'd expect in a mysterious or romantic story. He was rough, stubborn, and not exactly graceful—just a scruffy, no-nonsense painter. Today, people admire his art, even though back then, many found his personality unpleasant. Still, early in his life, he somehow found himself caught up in a strange and fascinating love story.

Who's to say what he was like when he was young? Maybe he was more charming or softer back then. Maybe the roughness he showed later in life came from pain or disappointment. We'll never really know.

So all we can do now is stick to the facts and leave the guessing to others.

When Schalken was still learning to paint under the famous Gerard Douw, he was a young man. Like many of his fellow Dutchmen, he had a calm nature, but that didn't mean he couldn't feel things deeply. In fact, it's well known that he had strong feelings for his teacher's beautiful niece.

Rose Velderkaust was still very young—not even seventeen yet—and, if the old stories are true, she had all the soft, delicate beauty of a fair-haired Flemish girl. Schalken hadn't been studying under Gerard Douw for long when he realized his feelings for Rose were growing stronger—stronger than what his calm, honest Dutch heart was used to. At the same time, he started to notice—or thought he did—that she seemed to like him back. That was all he needed to fully give his heart to her. He quickly fell as in love as any Dutchman could be.

It didn't take long for him to tell Rose how he felt, and she admitted she felt the same way. But Schalken was poor. He had no title or wealth to make up for it, so her uncle and guardian, Gerard Douw, wouldn't agree to a marriage that would drag Rose into a life of struggle with a nearly friendless young artist. Schalken was told he'd have to wait—until he had some success and a bit of luck. Then, maybe, Douw would at least consider letting him marry Rose.

Months passed, and Schalken worked harder than ever. Encouraged by Rose's smiles and support, he poured himself into his art. He made enough progress that it looked like his dreams could actually come true. He might even become a respected painter in just a few years.

But his steady path toward success and happiness was suddenly and strangely interrupted—so strangely, in fact, that no one could explain what happened. What followed felt like something from a ghost story.

One evening, Schalken stayed late in his master's studio. The other students had already left to enjoy the evening at the tavern, using the fading light as their excuse to leave. But Schalken wasn't working for fun—he was working for love. He was just sketching a design, which didn't require much light, unlike painting. At that time, he hadn't yet discovered his real talent with a paintbrush.

The drawing he was working on showed a bunch of creepy little demons tormenting a sweaty, drunk-looking Saint Anthony, who was lying in the middle of them with a big round belly. The scene was weird and silly, and Schalken kept trying to fix it. He erased and redrew parts over and over, but nothing seemed to make it better.

The big, old room was completely silent, and Schalken was alone. An hour went by—maybe two—

but he still wasn't happy with his sketch. The daylight had faded, and now it was almost dark. Frustrated, he stood staring at the unfinished drawing. One hand was tangled in his dark hair, and the other was holding the piece of charcoal that wasn't doing what he wanted. He rubbed it against his pants without thinking, leaving black smudges.

"Ugh!" he said out loud. "I wish that whole picture—demons, saint, and all—would just go straight to hell!"

Right then, someone laughed—a short, sharp laugh—right near his ear.

Startled, Schalken spun around and saw, for the first time, that someone had been watching him.

Just a few steps behind him stood a stranger. He looked like an older man. He wore a short cloak and a wide-brimmed hat with a pointed top. One hand, covered by a thick glove, held a long black cane with what looked like a gold handle that faintly shone in the dim light. Through the cloak, a shiny gold chain was visible on his chest.

The room was too dark to see him clearly, and the brim of his hat cast a shadow over his face, hiding any features. But some dark hair stuck out from under the hat, and the man's upright posture suggested he was probably no older than sixty.

The man's clothing gave him a serious, important look. But what really stood out—and made the artist freeze—was how completely still he stood, like a statue. It was so strange and unsettling that Schalken, who had been about to say something annoyed, held his tongue. Once he got over the shock, he politely asked the man to sit down and asked if he had a message for his teacher.

"Tell Gerard Douw," the man said, without moving at all, "that Mynheer Vanderhausen, from Rotterdam, wants to speak with him tomorrow evening at this same time, in this room, if possible. It's about something important. That is all. Good night."

Without waiting for a reply, the man turned quickly and walked out of the room so quietly that Schalken had no time to respond.

Feeling curious about where the man would go, Schalken rushed to the window that overlooked the door. Between the room and the front entrance was a hallway, so the artist had a moment to watch. But strangely, he never saw the man leave. There was only one way out, and the man hadn't taken it.

Had he disappeared? Was he hiding in the shadows, planning something bad? Schalken suddenly felt a cold fear he couldn't explain. He didn't want to stay alone in the room, but he was just as nervous about walking through the hallway. Still, he forced himself to leave, locked the door tightly behind him, and hurried through the dark passage without looking around, barely breathing until he was safely outside in the open air.

As the next evening came, Gerard Douw walked back and forth in his studio, deep in thought. "Mynheer Vanderhausen from Rotterdam?" he wondered. "I'd never even heard of him until yesterday. What could he want? Maybe he wants a portrait painted? Or he's bringing someone who wants to learn from me? Could he want me to look at a collection? No, it can't be an inheritance—nobody in Rotterdam would leave me money. Whatever it is, I guess I'll find out soon enough."

The day was ending, and all the other students had gone—except Schalken, still working at his easel. Douw walked around the room, stopping now and then to check a student's work or hum a tune he was trying to compose. Mostly, though, he kept going to the window to look out at the quiet street where his studio was.

"Didn't you say," Douw asked suddenly, "that the man said he'd come around seven, by the town hall clock?"

"It had just struck seven when I first saw him, sir," Schalken replied.

"Then he'll be here any minute," said Douw, checking his large, round pocket watch. "Mynheer Vanderhausen from Rotterdam—right?"

"That's the name."

"And he was an older man, well-dressed?"

"As far as I could see," said Schalken. "He wasn't exactly young, but he wasn't very old either. He wore expensive, serious-looking clothes—like someone important or wealthy."

Right then, the deep sound of the town hall clock rang seven times. Both men looked toward the door, waiting. When the last echo faded, Douw said, "Well, let's see if he actually shows up. If not, you can hang around for him, Godfrey—if you're that eager to meet some grumpy big-shot from Rotterdam. As for me, I think we already have plenty of important people here in Leyden."

Schalken gave a polite laugh, like he was supposed to. After a few quiet moments, Douw added, "What if this is all just a prank? Maybe Vankarp or someone like him is trying to mess with us. Honestly, I wish you had just hit that old 'burgomaster' or whatever he is. I bet after the third hit he'd be begging for mercy and calling you an old friend."

"Here he comes, sir," Schalken said softly.

Douw turned toward the door and immediately saw the same man who had visited Schalken the night before.

There was something serious and commanding about the man's presence that told Douw this wasn't a prank. This was someone important. Without hesitation, he took off his cap, greeted the stranger politely, and invited him to sit.

The visitor gave a quick wave, like a polite greeting, but he didn't take a seat.

"Am I speaking with Mynheer Vanderhausen from Rotterdam?" Gerard Douw asked.

"Yes, that's me," the stranger replied shortly.

"I understand you wish to speak with me," Douw continued, "and I'm here now, ready to listen."

"Is that man trustworthy?" Vanderhausen asked, pointing toward Schalken, who was standing a short distance behind his master.

"Absolutely," Douw replied.

"Then give him this box," said Vanderhausen, handing over a small case about nine inches wide. "Tell him to take it to the nearest jeweler or goldsmith and get the contents valued. He should return with a written certificate."

Douw was surprised by how heavy the box was and by how suddenly it had been handed to him. Still, he passed it along to Schalken and repeated the instructions.

Schalken carefully hid the box under his cloak and quickly made his way through a few narrow streets until he reached a corner shop owned by a Jewish goldsmith.

He brought the man into the back room and showed him the box. Under the lamp's light, it appeared to be covered in old, scratched-up lead, almost white with age. With some effort, they peeled away the outer layer, revealing a box made of dark, incredibly hard wood. They opened that, removed a few layers of linen, and found tightly packed gold bars inside—solid, shining, and perfect.

The little Jew examined each piece of gold like it was a rare treat, testing it with great care and whispering to himself with each one: "Mein Gott, so perfect! Not a bit of impurity—beautiful, beautiful!"

When he was done, he wrote a certificate confirming that the gold was worth several thousand rix-dollars. With the paper tucked safely into his coat and the gold securely hidden again, Schalken made his way back. When he returned to the studio, he found his master and the strange visitor deep in conversation.

Not long after Schalken had left, Vanderhausen began to speak to Douw:

"I won't stay long tonight, so I'll get straight to the point. About four months ago, you visited Rotterdam. While there, I saw your niece, Rose Velderkaust, in the Church of St. Lawrence. I want to marry her. If I can prove I'm extremely wealthy—far richer than any other suitor you've considered—I expect you to help me. If you agree, you must say so right away. I don't have time to waste on delays or second thoughts."

Douw was shocked by this sudden proposal, but he didn't show it. Part of him wanted to be polite, but another part of him felt something cold and uncomfortable standing near this man—like being close to something your body just naturally fears.

After a few nervous throat-clears, Douw replied, "There's no doubt that such a marriage would bring wealth and status to my niece. But you must understand, she has her own opinions. She may not go along with something just because we think it's good for her."

"Don't try to fool me, Painter," Vanderhausen said. "You are her guardian. Her future is in your hands. She can be mine—if you agree."

He stepped forward slightly, and though Douw didn't know why, he found himself silently hoping Schalken would come back soon.

"I wish," said the strange man, "to show you right away that I'm wealthy, and that I'll be generous with your niece. The young man will return shortly with a box worth five times more than what she could ever expect as a marriage gift. I'll leave it with you, along with her dowry, and you can manage the money in whatever way helps her most. It will belong only to her for as long as she lives. Is that generous enough?"

Douw agreed and quietly thought his niece had been incredibly lucky. He figured this man must be very rich and generous—and that such an offer, even if made by someone a little strange, shouldn't be ignored.

Rose didn't have a big dowry. In fact, she had almost nothing except what her uncle had given her. And she couldn't argue that the man was beneath her socially—she came from a simple background herself. As for other concerns, Gerard had already decided, as most men of his time would, not to take them too seriously.

"Sir," Gerard said politely, "your offer is very generous, and my only hesitation comes from the fact that I don't know anything about your background. But I assume you can clear that up easily?"

"As for my status," said the stranger sharply, "you'll just have to accept what I choose to share. Don't ask too many questions—you won't learn more than I want you to know. If you're honorable, my word should be enough. If you're greedy, let the gold speak for me."

"A stubborn man," thought Douw. "Still, all things considered, I think I can safely accept him as a match for my niece. Even if she were my own daughter, I'd probably do the same. But I won't agree too quickly."

"You won't agree too quickly," repeated Vanderhausen, oddly echoing Douw's private thought. "But you will agree if it becomes necessary. And I say it is. If the gold satisfies you, and you want this offer to stay on the table, then before I leave this room, you must sign this paper."

He handed Gerard a document. It said that Gerard agreed to marry Rose Velderkaust to Wilken Vanderhausen of Rotterdam within one week.

While Gerard was reading it, Schalken returned with the box and the written appraisal from the jeweler. He handed them to Vanderhausen and was about to leave when the stranger told him to stay. Vanderhausen gave both the box and the note to Gerard, who checked them carefully and saw they were indeed worth a great deal.

"Are you satisfied?" asked the stranger.

"I would prefer one more day to think it over," said the painter.

"Not even an hour," the man replied calmly.

"Alright," said Douw. "I agree. It's a deal."

"Then sign now," Vanderhausen insisted. "I'm tired."

He pulled out a small writing kit, and Gerard signed the paper.

"Let this young man witness the contract," said the stranger.

Without realizing it, Schalken signed the document that gave the woman he loved to someone else.

Once it was done, the stranger folded the paper and tucked it away inside his coat.

"I'll visit your house tomorrow at nine in the evening, Gerard Douw," he said. "I want to see the young woman we agreed upon. Goodbye."

With that, Vanderhausen walked stiffly but quickly out of the room.

Schalken had rushed to the window, hoping to see him leave. But the man never came out through the door. That only made Schalken feel more nervous and suspicious. He and Gerard walked home together, both deep in their own thoughts—some hopeful, some worried.

But Schalken had no idea how close he was to losing everything he hoped for. Gerard didn't know about the love between his niece and his student—and even if he had, it's unlikely he would've let it get in the way of Vanderhausen's wishes.

Back then, marriages were mostly about money and social status—not love. To Rose's uncle, it would've seemed silly to think real feelings had anything to do with marriage, just like it would seem odd to write legal contracts in flowery, romantic language.

Still, Gerard Douw didn't tell his niece what he'd arranged. It wasn't because he thought she'd argue, but because he was embarrassed. He realized that if she asked what her future husband looked like, he wouldn't be able to describe him—he hadn't even seen the man's face. He wouldn't be able to recognize him at all.

The next day, after lunch, Douw called Rose over. He looked her over proudly, then smiled warmly and said, "Rose, that face of yours will bring you good fortune." Rose blushed. "It's rare to see a pretty face like yours paired with such a sweet nature. That combination is impossible to resist. Trust me, you'll be married soon. But enough talk—I'm short on time. Get the large room ready by eight tonight, and make sure supper's served at nine. I have a guest coming. And Rose, make yourself look nice. I don't want him thinking we're poor or messy."

With that, he left and went to the studio where his students usually worked.

As evening came, Douw stopped Schalken, who was about to head back to his cold, shabby lodgings. He invited him to come home and eat supper with him, Rose, and Vanderhausen.

Schalken accepted, of course, and soon he and his teacher were in the nicely decorated room, waiting for their strange visitor.

A warm fire burned in the big fireplace. Off to the side, an old table with carved legs had been set up for supper, and tall-backed chairs were arranged neatly around it. They weren't pretty, but they were comfortable.

The little group—Rose, her uncle, and Schalken—waited nervously for the guest to arrive.

At last, the clock struck nine. There was a knock at the front door, which was quickly answered. Then they heard slow, heavy steps coming up the stairs, crossing the hallway, and finally the door to the room creaked open.

The person who walked in shocked the calm Dutch group—and nearly made Rose scream. It was the man they knew as Mynheer Vanderhausen. His posture, his walk, and his clothes were just the same, but no one in the room had ever seen his face before.

The man stood in the doorway, fully visible now. He wore a dark cloak that came down just above the knees. His legs were covered in dark purple stockings, and his shoes had matching purple decorations. Under his cloak was an outfit made of some very dark material, maybe black fur. His hands were covered in thick leather gloves that reached high up his wrists. In one hand, he held his walking stick and hat, and his other arm hung stiffly by his side. Long, gray hair fell from his head and rested against a stiff white collar that completely hid his neck.

So far, everything seemed strange but normal. But then came the face.

His skin had a sickly, bluish-gray color, like someone who had taken too much poisonous medicine. His eyes were huge, with the whites showing clearly all around the irises, making him look mad—and they didn't move. They were completely still, like glass. His nose looked normal, but his mouth was twisted to one side, revealing two long, dark fangs that hung down from the top of his mouth past his lower lip. His lips were nearly black, like the rest of his face. Altogether, his expression was so evil, so inhuman, it seemed like something out of a nightmare. It was the kind of face you'd expect to see on the rotting body of a criminal who had been left hanging on a gallows—only now possessed by a demon.

The strange visitor made sure to keep as much of his skin covered as possible and never took off his gloves the entire time he was there.

He stood silently at the doorway for a few moments until Gerard Douw finally managed to welcome him. Without a word, the stranger gave a small nod and stepped into the room.

There was something very strange—almost frightening—about how he moved. It wasn't something you could easily explain, but it was as if his body was being controlled by someone unfamiliar with how human limbs are supposed to work.

Vanderhausen barely spoke during his visit, which lasted less than thirty minutes. Even Gerard, the host, could hardly bring himself to say more than the few polite things needed. In fact, the stranger's presence made everyone so nervous that it wouldn't have taken much for them to run screaming from the room.

Still, they were able to notice two very strange things about him. First, he never blinked—not once. His eyelids didn't even twitch. Second, his chest didn't move at all. There was no sign that he was breathing. These two details, though they may not sound that shocking when described, were deeply disturbing to watch in person.

At last, Vanderhausen left, and the small group was more than relieved to hear the front door close behind him.

"Dear uncle," Rose said, "what a terrifying man! I wouldn't want to see him again for all the money in the world!"

"Don't be silly, girl," Douw replied, though he didn't feel very calm himself. "A man can be as ugly as sin, and still be a good person. That's worth more than a pretty face and fancy perfume. Rose, it's true he doesn't have your looks, but he's rich and generous. Even if he were ten times uglier—"

"Which is hard to imagine," Rose interrupted.

"—those two qualities would make up for his looks," her uncle continued. "They might not change his face, but they'd help you overlook it."

"Uncle," Rose said, "when I saw him standing there, I couldn't stop thinking he looked just like that creepy wooden figure in St. Laurence's church back in Rotterdam—the one that used to scare me."

Gerard laughed, though he secretly agreed. Still, he wanted to stop her from making fun of the man she was supposed to marry. Even so, he was quietly happy to see she wasn't feeling the same fear of Vanderhausen that he and his student Schalken had.

The next morning, fancy gifts started arriving at the house—silks, velvet, jewelry—all for Rose. A sealed packet also arrived, addressed to Gerard Douw. Inside was a formal marriage contract between Wilken Vanderhausen of Boom Quay in Rotterdam and Rose Velderkaust of Leyden, Gerard's niece. It included generous promises of money and property for Rose, even more than Douw had expected. All of it would be managed by Gerard himself to make sure Rose was well taken care of.

This story has no dramatic speeches, no noble self-sacrifices, no weeping lovers. It's not romantic. It's a tale of cold decisions, carelessness, and self-interest. Less than a week after the first visit, the wedding took place—and Schalken had to watch the woman he loved be taken away by the man he feared.

Schalken didn't come to the studio for a few days. When he finally returned, he wasn't cheerful, but he worked harder than ever. Love had been replaced by a new goal: success.

Several months passed, and to Gerard Douw's surprise, he still hadn't heard a single word from his niece or her new husband, even though they had promised to stay in touch. He had even expected someone to collect the interest from the money that had been left in his care, but no one ever came. Gerard started to feel seriously worried.

He had the address Vanderhausen had given in Rotterdam, so after thinking it over, he decided to travel there himself. It was a short trip, and he hoped he could check on Rose and make sure everything was okay. He truly cared about her and felt it was his duty to look after her well-being.

But the trip didn't help. No one in Rotterdam had ever heard of anyone named Vanderhausen. Gerard went door to door along Boom Quay, asking questions, but no one could tell him anything. He had no choice but to return home, just as confused as before.

When he got back, he went to the place that had rented the carriage used for the wedding trip. The driver told him that they had traveled slowly and reached the outskirts of Rotterdam late at night. But before they entered the city, about a mile outside, they were stopped by a small group of men standing in the middle of the road. These men wore old-fashioned clothing and had pointed beards and mustaches. They were carrying a large, old-style litter, which they set down in front of the carriage.

The groom stepped out first and helped Rose out. She was crying and looked very upset. The couple climbed into the litter together. The men then picked it up and carried it away toward the city. Within a few moments, the darkness swallowed them, and the driver couldn't see them anymore.

Later, when the driver checked inside the coach, he found a bag of money—more than enough to cover the cost of the trip. That was the last he ever saw of Vanderhausen or Rose.

The whole mystery deeply troubled Gerard. He was sure that Vanderhausen had tricked him somehow, but he didn't know why. Something about that man's face had always seemed evil. And every day without news from Rose only made his fears grow stronger.

He also missed her bright and cheerful presence more than he had expected. To help chase away the loneliness, he often invited Schalken to eat supper with him, just to have someone there to talk to.

One evening, Gerard and Schalken had finished dinner and were sitting quietly by the fire. They had slipped into that thoughtful silence that sometimes happens after a good meal, when suddenly there was a loud pounding at the front door—like someone was throwing themselves against it again and again.

A servant quickly went to see what was going on. They heard him calling out, asking who was there, but got no answer. The banging didn't stop. Then they heard the front door open, followed by fast footsteps coming up the stairs.

Schalken reached for his sword and moved toward the door. But before he could reach it, the door burst open—and Rose ran into the room.

She looked wild, exhausted, and pale with fear. But what shocked them as much as her sudden return was what she was wearing. She had on a long white wool robe that closed at the neck and reached all the way to the floor. It was dirty and wrinkled, like she had been traveling for days.

She had barely made it into the room when she collapsed on the floor, unconscious. It took a while, but they finally brought her back. And as soon as she opened her eyes, she shouted in a voice full of panic:

"Please, get me some wine—hurry, or something terrible will happen!"

Startled by how desperate she sounded, they quickly gave her some wine. She drank it so fast and eagerly that it left them surprised. But right after finishing it, she cried out again, just as urgently, "Food, food, now—or I'll die!"

There was some roasted meat on the table, and Schalken moved to cut a portion for her. But before he could, Rose grabbed it with her bare hands, tore off chunks with her teeth, and devoured it like she hadn't eaten in days.

Once her hunger had eased a bit, she suddenly seemed to realize how strange her behavior had been—or perhaps darker thoughts came flooding back to her—because she burst into tears and wrung her hands.

"Please, send for a priest," she said through her sobs. "I'm not safe until he comes—please hurry!"

Gerard Douw immediately sent someone to fetch a minister. He also offered his own bedroom to Rose, and persuaded her to go rest there. She agreed, but only on one condition—that they wouldn't leave her alone.

"Oh, I wish the holy man were here already," she whispered. "He's the only one who can help me. The dead and the living can't be together—God doesn't allow it."

With those strange words, she let them lead her toward the bedroom. "Don't leave me," she begged. "If you do, I'm lost forever."

To get to Douw's bedroom, they had to pass through a large connecting room. Both men carried candles, casting light around as they entered. But just as they were about to step into the big room, Rose froze. In a trembling whisper, full of fear, she gasped, "Oh God—he's here! There he goes—look!"

She pointed at the doorway ahead. Schalken thought he saw a blurry, shadowy figure slide silently into the next room. He lifted his candle and drew his sword, rushing forward to catch a better look. But when he stepped inside, the room was empty—only the furniture remained. Still, he couldn't shake the feeling that something, or someone, had just passed through there.

A wave of fear hit him, and sweat rolled down his face. Then he heard Rose crying out, even more desperately now, begging them not to leave her alone for a single moment.

"I saw him," she said, her voice shaking. "He's here—I know it. He's beside me, in this room. Please, for God's sake, don't leave me!"

They convinced her to lie down on the bed, but she kept pleading with them to stay close. She muttered strange, broken sentences again and again, like, "The dead and the living can't be one—God forbids it!" and "Let the sleepless rest—let the sleepwalkers sleep."

She kept rambling like this until the priest finally arrived.

Douw, understandably, started to worry that his niece had gone mad—whether from fear or from something worse. The time she appeared, the state she was in, and her strange behavior all made him wonder if she had escaped from some kind of asylum and feared being dragged back. He decided he would call a doctor—but not until the minister had done what she'd so desperately asked for. Until then, he didn't dare question her, afraid it might only upset her more.

The priest soon arrived. He was an old man with a serious face, someone Gerard Douw respected deeply—not because he was warm or friendly, but because he was a strong debater. He was known for his sharp mind and spotless behavior, though he was more feared than loved. As soon as he entered the room that connected to where Rose was lying, she asked him to pray for her. She said she was in Satan's power and that only Heaven could save her.

To help you picture the scene clearly: the priest and Schalken were in the outer room. Rose was lying in the bedroom with the door wide open, and her uncle Gerard was standing next to her bed because she had begged him not to leave. There was one candle burning near the bed and three candles in the outer room.

The priest cleared his throat to begin the prayer, but before he could start, a sudden gust of air blew out the only candle in the bedroom. Rose cried out quickly, "Godfrey, bring another candle! It's not safe in the dark!"

Without thinking, Gerard stepped into the next room to get one. In a panic, Rose screamed, "Oh God! Don't go, uncle!" and jumped out of bed to try and grab his arm.

But it was too late. As soon as he crossed the doorway, the door between the rooms slammed shut with a loud bang, like it had been thrown closed by a strong wind.

Gerard and Schalken rushed to open it, pushing with all their strength, but the door wouldn't budge. Then came the screaming. Rose cried out again and again, her voice full of pure terror. They kept trying to break the door down, but nothing worked.

They didn't hear any struggle inside, but her screams grew louder and more desperate. At the same time, they heard the sound of the window bolts being unlocked and the window scraping open.

Then came one final scream—so loud, so long, and so full of fear that it didn't even sound human. And then… silence.

A few seconds later, they heard light footsteps crossing the floor, moving from the bed toward the window. Right then, the door suddenly gave way, and both men nearly fell into the room from the force of their pushing.

But the room was empty.

The window stood wide open. Schalken climbed onto a chair and looked out toward the street and the canal below. He didn't see anyone, but he thought he saw the water below rippling in large, slow circles—like something big had just fallen in.

They never found Rose again. No one ever uncovered the truth about what happened to her—or who that strange man really was. No clues were ever found to explain any of it.

But one event afterward stayed with Schalken forever. Even if no one else believed it, he never forgot.

THE WATERS OF THE BROAD CANAL BENEATH SETTLING RING AFTER RING IN HEAVY CIRCULAR RIPPLES.

Years later, long after everything had happened, Schalken was living far away when he got news that his father had died and was going to be buried on a set date in a church in Rotterdam. The funeral would require a long journey, and not many people were expected to attend. Schalken barely made it to Rotterdam late on the day of the funeral. When he arrived, the procession hadn't yet reached the church.

He walked to the church, which was already open. They had been told the funeral was happening, and the burial vault had already been opened. The man in charge of the crypt—like a church caretaker or sexton—saw Schalken, who was well-dressed and clearly there for the funeral. The caretaker invited him to come sit by the fire he had lit in a nearby room, as he often did in winter during events like this. The room connected to the vault below by a flight of stairs.

Schalken sat with him in the warm room. The caretaker tried to make conversation, but when Schalken didn't really respond, he gave up and relaxed with his pipe and drink. Schalken, exhausted from his long trip and heavy thoughts, slowly drifted off into a deep sleep.

He was woken by someone gently shaking his shoulder. At first, he thought it was the caretaker, but the old man was no longer there. Schalken sat up and looked around. What he saw made him freeze—a woman was standing nearby, wearing a light muslin gown, part of which covered her head like a veil. She held a small lamp in one hand and was walking toward the stairs that led down into the vaults.

Even though he felt nervous, he couldn't stop himself from following her. When she reached the top of the stairs, she turned around and looked at him. The light from her lamp lit up her face. It was Rose Velderkaust—his first love.

Her face wasn't frightening or sad. Instead, she wore the same playful smile he had fallen in love with years ago. Filled with a mix of wonder and fear, Schalken followed her down the stairs. She led him through a narrow hallway and, to his surprise, into a room that looked just like something from one of Gerard Douw's paintings—an old-style Dutch bedroom.

The room was filled with expensive antique furniture, and in one corner stood a heavy four-poster bed with dark curtains. Rose kept glancing back at him, always with that same smile. She walked to the bed, pulled back the curtains, and held the lamp toward the figure inside.

Schalken's heart nearly stopped.

Sitting upright in the bed was the terrifying, pale, and devilish figure of Vanderhausen.

Schalken collapsed on the floor, unconscious.

He was found the next morning by workers who had come to seal off the vault. He was lying in a large room that hadn't been used in years, next to an old coffin that rested on small stone stands meant to keep animals away.

Schalken always believed what he saw that night was real. Not only did he never forget it, but he also painted a haunting picture shortly afterward. The painting showed all the eerie details in his unique style, but more importantly, it captured the face of Rose Velderkaust—

the woman he had once loved, and whose strange fate was never explained.

SHE DREW THE CURTAINS.

The painting shows an old stone room, like one you might find in an ancient cathedral. It's dimly lit by a small lamp held by a woman—the same one described earlier. In the background, to the left of anyone looking at the picture, stands a man who looks like he just woke up. His hand rests on his sword, and his body language shows that he's alarmed. He's lit only by the dying glow of a wood or coal fire.

The whole painting is a great example of Schalken's unique skill at using light and shadow to create mood, one of the reasons he became such a famous artist in his country. This story is based on an old legend, and if you noticed that we didn't exaggerate or add extra drama where we could have, it's because we wanted to share a curious tale that people have long connected to Schalken's life—not just a made-up ghost story.

The End

Thank You for Reading

Dear Reader,

We hope this timeless classic has sparked your imagination and enriched your literary journey. Now that you've turned the final page, we want to share a vision for the future of reading—one where every classic you've ever wanted to explore is at your fingertips, in a format that best suits your life.

We'd like to invite you to gain immediate, unlimited digital & audiobook access to hundreds of the most treasured literary classics ever written—along with the option to secure deluxe paperback, hardcover & box set editions at printing cost. Together, we can spark a new global literary renaissance alongside our small, independent publishing house called "The Library of Alexandria."

Thousands of years ago, the Library of Alexandria stood as a beacon of knowledge—until it was lost to history. We aim to reignite that spirit of preservation and discovery right now, in the modern age—only this time, it's accessible to all, in every language and every format.

Picture a world where every timeless classic, novel, poem, or philosophical treatise is not only available to read but also updated for today's readers—modernized, translated into any language or dialect, and ready to enjoy in any format you choose, whether that is in an eBook, audiobook, paperback, or deluxe hardcover & box set version a printing cost.

By joining our movement to rebuild the modern Library of Alexandria, you become part of an unprecedented mission to offer:

- **Unlimited Audiobook & eBook Access to the Greatest Classics of All Time**

  Instantly explore thousands of legendary works, from Plato and Shakespeare to Jane Austen and Leo Tolstoy. All are instantly ready to read or listen to, giving you a complete literary universe at your fingertips.

- **Paperback & Deluxe Editions at Printing Costs:**

  Purchase any title in a paperback, deluxe hardbound, or deluxe boxset edition at printing costs, shipped right to your doorstep. Curate your personal library of Alexandria with editions worthy of display—crafted to last, designed to captivate, and delivered straight to your door.

- **Modern translations for Contemporary Readers in all languages and dialects**

  Discover a vast selection of classics reimagined in clear, current language—no more struggling with outdated phrases or obscure references. Next to the original versions, we aim to offer translations in as many languages and dialects as possible.

  As we continue our translation efforts and add new languages, readers everywhere can connect with these works as if they were written today. By bridging linguistic divides, you're contributing to ensuring that these timeless stories become more meaningful, accessible, and inspiring for people across the globe.

- **Your Personal Library of Alexandria:**

  Over the months and years, you'll curate a unique physical archive of classics—each volume a testament to your taste, curiosity, and love of knowledge. It's not just about owning books—it's about curating a cultural legacy you'll cherish and pass down for generations to come.

- **Join a Global Literary Renaissance:**

  Your support fuels an ongoing mission: allowing us to reinvest in offering deluxe print editions (including special boxsets) at their true cost, broaden the range of available formats and translations, and extend the reach of these works to new audiences worldwide. By joining today, you're not just preserving a legacy of masterpieces; you set in motion a powerful wave of literary accessibility.

We are more than a publisher—we're a movement, and we can't do it alone. Your support lets us scale our mission, preserving and reimagining history's greatest works for tomorrow's readers.

Become a Torchbearer of knowledge.

Thank you for picking up this book and allowing us into your literary journey. As you turn the pages, know that you're part of something larger: a global effort to keep these stories alive, share their wisdom across borders and generations, and spark a true cultural revival for the modern era.

If this resonates with you—please consider taking the next step by visiting:

www.libraryofalexandria.com

With gratitude and a shared love of knowledge,

The Modern Library of Alexandria Team

Visit:

www.libraryofalexandria.com

Or scan the code below:

www.ingramcontent.com/pod-product-compliance
Lightning Source LLC
Chambersburg PA
CBHW010356310726
48979CB00006B/1054

* 9 7 8 1 8 0 6 2 9 1 4 0 3 *